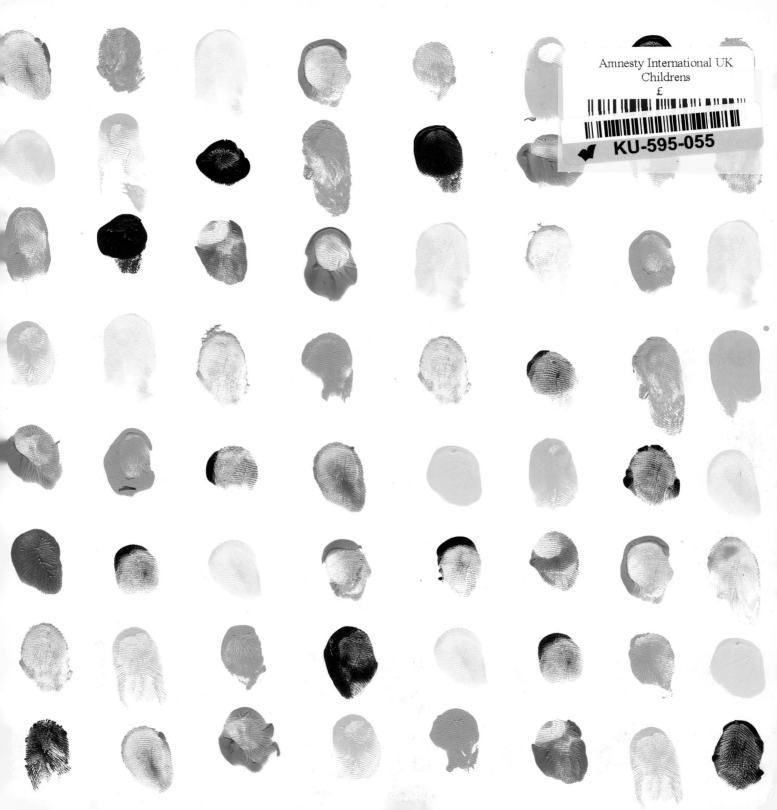

Amnesty International UK
Childrens
£

KU-595-055

IT'S THAT TIME AGAIN.

ARE YOU READY?

TAP THAT GREY SPOT. JUST A LITTLE,
TO SEE WHAT HAPPENS.

THERE THEY ARE!

BUT DON'T THEY SEEM A BIT SHY?
TAP IT AGAIN. TAP, TAP, TAP.

HERE THEY COME!

BUT THERE ARE A FEW STILL MISSING.
TRY TAPPING JUST ONE MORE TIME.

FiNALLY! THEY'RE ALL HERE. SO NOW . . .

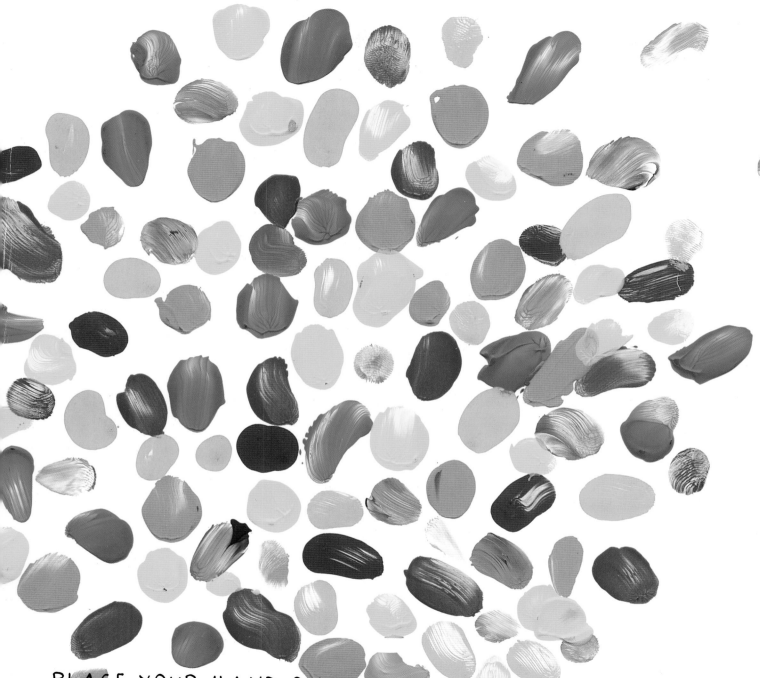

PLACE YOUR HAND ON THE PAGE, CLOSE YOUR EYES, AND COUNT TO FIVE.

YES! YOU'VE GOT THE MAGIC TOUCH!

LET'S MIX IT UP!

WITH ONE FINGER TAKE A LITTLE BIT OF THE BLUE . . .

AND JUST TOUCH THE YELLOW. RUB iT . . . GENTLY . . .

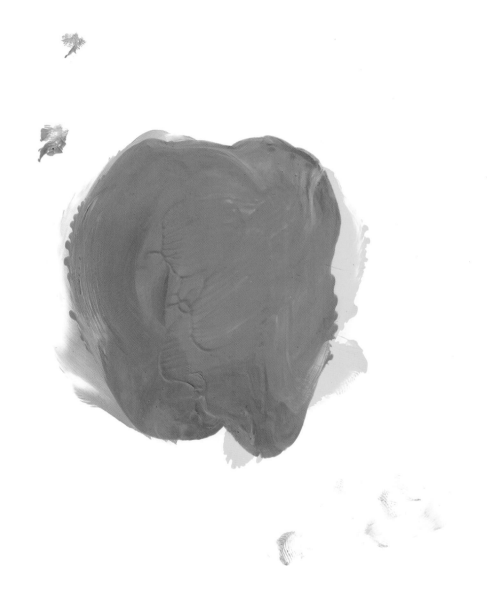

SEE?

NOW TAKE A LiTTLE BiT OF THE RED . . .

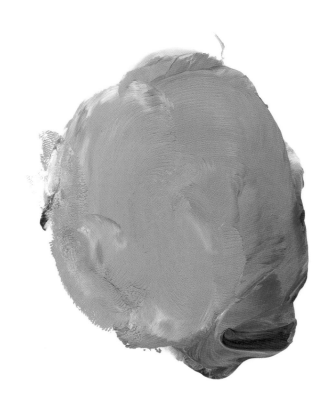

AND RUB IT ON THE BLUE.

OK?

TRY TAKING SOME OF THAT YELLOW . . .

AND SMUDGING iT ON THE RED.

GREAT! CAN YOU REMEMBER ALL THAT?

NOW LET'S HAVE SOME FUN.

DO YOU WANT TO GO ON? OK!

SO SHAKE THE BOOK REALLY HARD.

WHAT DO YOU THINK WILL HAPPEN?

RIGHT!

NOW TRY TILTING THE BOOK TO THE RIGHT.

WHAT DO YOU THiNK WiLL HAPPEN?

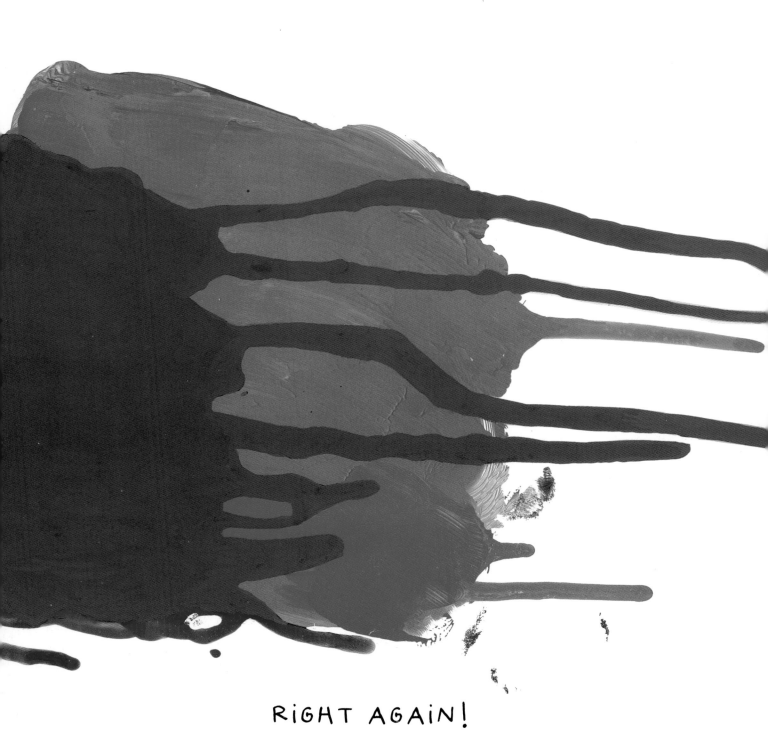

RIGHT AGAIN!

CLOSE THE BOOK AND PUSH DOWN REALLY HARD . . .

SO THE COLOURS SQUISH TOGETHER. . . .

YOU THOUGHT SO?

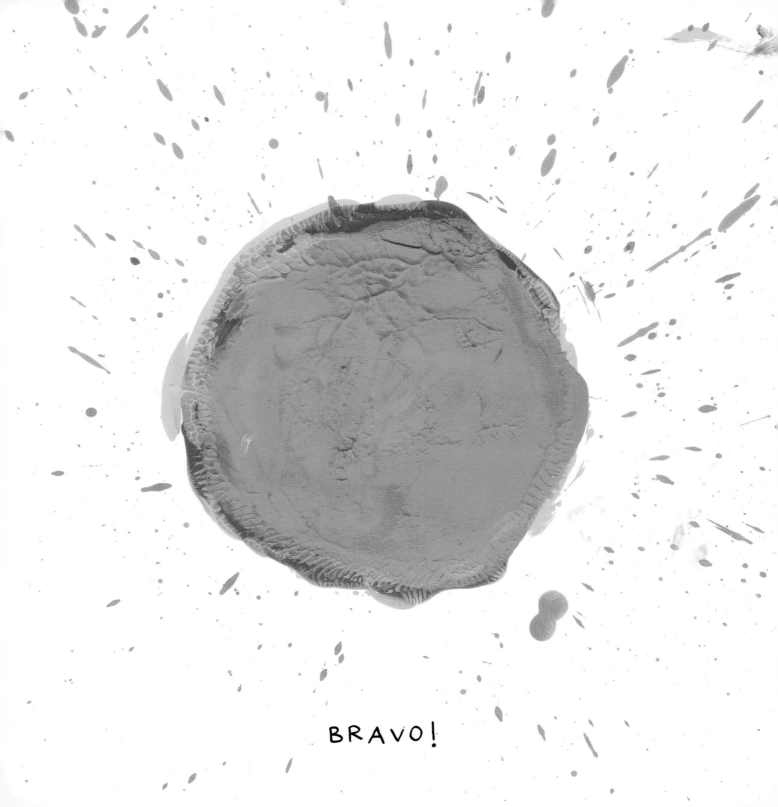

BRAVO!

IF YOU RUB THE TWO COLOURS TOGETHER REALLY HARD . .

THEN WHAT HAPPENS?

YOU'VE GOT IT!

AND TO TURN ALL OF THOSE DOTS TO GREEN,

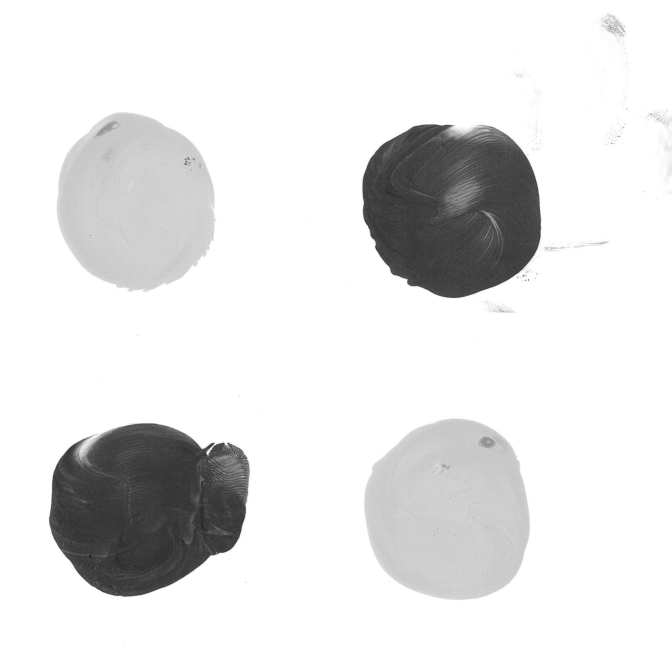

WHAT DO YOU HAVE TO DO?

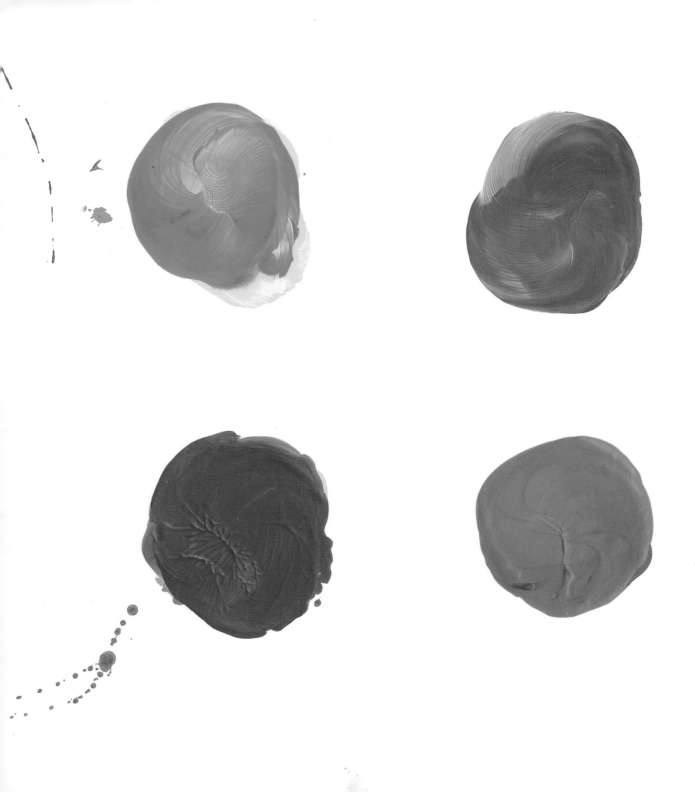

YES! WELL DONE!

MORE?

WHITE MAKES COLOURS LIGHTER.

GO AHEAD, TRY IT!

SEE?

AND BLACK MAKES THEM DARKER.

TRY iT AGAiN!

THERE! MAKES SENSE, DOESN'T IT?

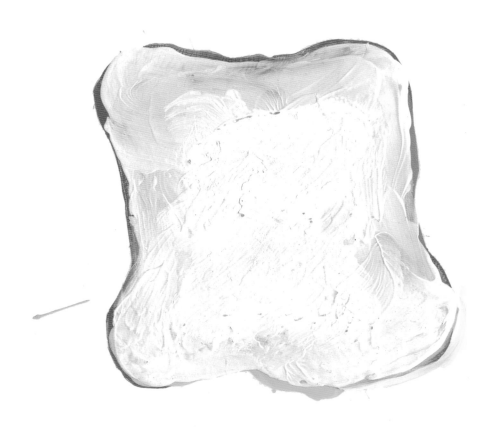

SO iF YOU SMOOSH THESE TWO PAGES TOGETHER . . .

(JUST CLOSE THE BOOK QUICKLY!)

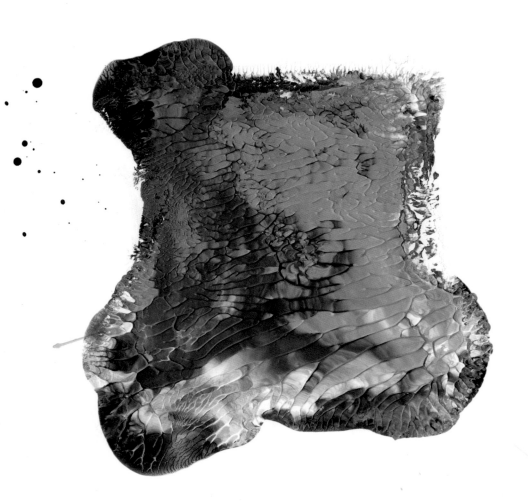

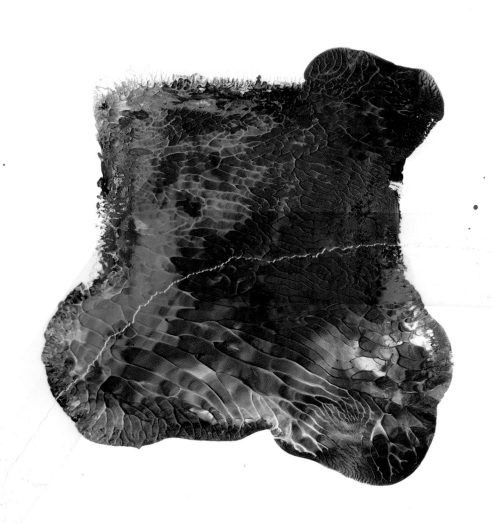

. . . THiS iS WHAT WiLL HAPPEN!

THAT'S IT. YOU'VE GOT IT. ALL DONE!

JUST ONE MORE THING:

PLACE YOUR HAND ON THE PAGE AND . . .

COUNT TO FIVE . . .

GOOD-BYE!

ON YOUR OWN NOW!

LOOK,

PLAY,

AND

Mix iT UP!

First published in the United States of America in 2014 by Chronicle Books LLC.

Originally published in France in 2014 by Bayard Éditions under the title "COULEURS."

Text and illustration copyright © 2014 by Bayard Éditions.

Translation copyright © 2014 by Chronicle Books LLC.

All rights reserved. No part of this book may be reproduced in any form without written permission from the publisher.

ISBN 978-1-4521-4057-5

Manufactured in China.

Translated by Christopher Franceschelli.
Original French Edition Design by Sandrine Granon.
Chronicle Books edition design by Amelia Mack.
Typeset in HervéTulletWhimsy.
The illustrations in this book were rendered in paint.

10 9 8 7 6 5 4 3 2 1

Handprint Books
An imprint of Chronicle Books LLC
680 Second Street
San Francisco, CA 94107

Distributed in Europe by
Abrams & Chronicle Books Limited
72-82 Rosebery Avenue
London, EC1R 4RW

www.chroniclekids.com
www.chroniclebooks.com/mixitup
www.herve-tullet.com